Black History Makers

Civil-Rights Activists

Debbie Foy

PowerKiDS press
New York

Published in 2012 by The Rosen Publishing Group, Inc.
29 East 21st Street, New York, NY 10010

Copyright © 2012 Wayland/The Rosen Publishing Group, Inc.

All rights reserved. No part of this book may be reproduced in any form without permission in writing from the publisher, except by a reviewer.

Editor: Katie Woolley, Jennifer Way
Designer: Tim Mayer, MayerMedia
Consultant: Mia Morris, Black History Month Web Site

Picture Acknowledgments: cover, p. 16 Ernst Haas/Ernst Haas Collection/Getty Images; p. 20 Gregory Pace/BEI/Rex Features; title page, pp. 6, 10 Library of Congress. 19 Wall McNamee/Corbis; contents page, p. 17 Francis Miller/Time–Life Pictures/Getty Images; p. 4 iStockphoto; pp. 5, 22 (top right) Shutterstock; pp. 7, 11 MPI/Getty Images; p. 8 Mary Evans Picture Library/Alamy; p. 9 Nils Jorgensen/Rex Features; p. 12 Wisconsin Historical Society/Everett Collection/Rex Features; pp. 13, 14, 15, Courtesy Everett Collection/Rex Features; p. 18 Jon Hrusa/EPA/Corbis; p. 21 Foto24/Gaho Images/Getty Images; p. 22 (bottom right) Arno Burgi/EPA/Corbis; p. 22 (top left) Bettmann/Corbis; p. 22 (center) Eric Fougere/VIP Images/Corbis; p. 22 (bottom left) Photos 12/Alamy.

Library of Congress Cataloging-in-Publication Data

Foy, Debbie.
 Civil-rights activists / by Debbie Foy. — 1st ed.
  p. cm. — (Black history makers)
 Includes index.
 ISBN 978-1-4488-6638-0 (library binding) — ISBN 978-1-4488-7054-7 (pbk.) — ISBN 978-1-4488-7055-4 (6-pack)
 1. African American civil rights workers — Biography — Juvenile literature. 2. Civil rights workers — United States — Biography — Juvenile literature. 3. African Americans — Civil rights — History — Juvenile literature. 4. Civil rights workers — Biography — Juvenile literature. 5. Human rights workers — Biography — Juvenile literature. I. Title.
 E185.96.F69 2012
 323.092'2—dc23
 [B]
                    2011029076

Manufactured in Malaysia

WEB SITES:

Due to the changing nature of Internet links, PowerKids Press has developed an online list of Web sites related to the subject of this book. This site is updated regularly. Please use this link to access the list:
www.powerkidslinks.com/blackhist/civil/

CPSIA Compliance Information: Batch #WW2102PK: For Further Information contact Rosen Publishing, New York, New York at 1-800-237-9932

CONTENTS

What Is an Activist? 4

Sojourner Truth
Feminist and Abolitionist 6

Harriet Tubman
Underground Railroad Conductor 7

Mary Seacole
The War Nurse 8

Frederick Douglass
Inspirational Speaker 10

Marcus Garvey
Back-to-Africa Movement 11

Rosa Parks
Mother of the Civil Rights Movement 12

Malcolm X
Black Nationalist 14

Martin Luther King Jr.
Civil Rights Hero 16

Archbishop Desmond Tutu
Antiapartheid Activist 18

Oprah Winfrey
Modern Campaigner 20

Other Activists 22

Timeline 23

Legacy 23

Glossary 24

Index 24

What Is an Activist?

Activists are people who try to persuade others to change things for the good. Their campaigns take place either through public speaking, protests, or **petitions**. Activistists might support causes such as civil rights or protest against environmental issues, racism, or **oppression**. Most campaigning is peaceful but sometimes it can become violent.

Campaigns for Freedom

When slavery began in North America in the 1600s, slaves were forced to work for white slaveholders on large **plantations**. They were unpaid and often treated brutally. Between 1600 and 1800, millions of Africans were shipped to North America to serve as slaves. American activists such as Harriet Tubman (page 7) used the Underground Railroad to help slaves flee the Southern states. **Abolitionists** such as Sojourner Truth (page 6) and Frederick Douglass (page 10) devoted their lives to campaigning peacefully against slavery.

Peaceful protests that use nonviolence are respected around the world.

THE ERA OF BLACK POWER

The Civil War (1861–1865) was sparked by slavery in the Southern States, which left the United States to form the Confederate States of America. After the war, these states rejoined the United States and promised to end racial **segregation**, but this promise was not fulfilled. Activists such as Malcolm X (page 14) and Martin Luther King Jr. (page 16) campaigned and changed the course of black history.

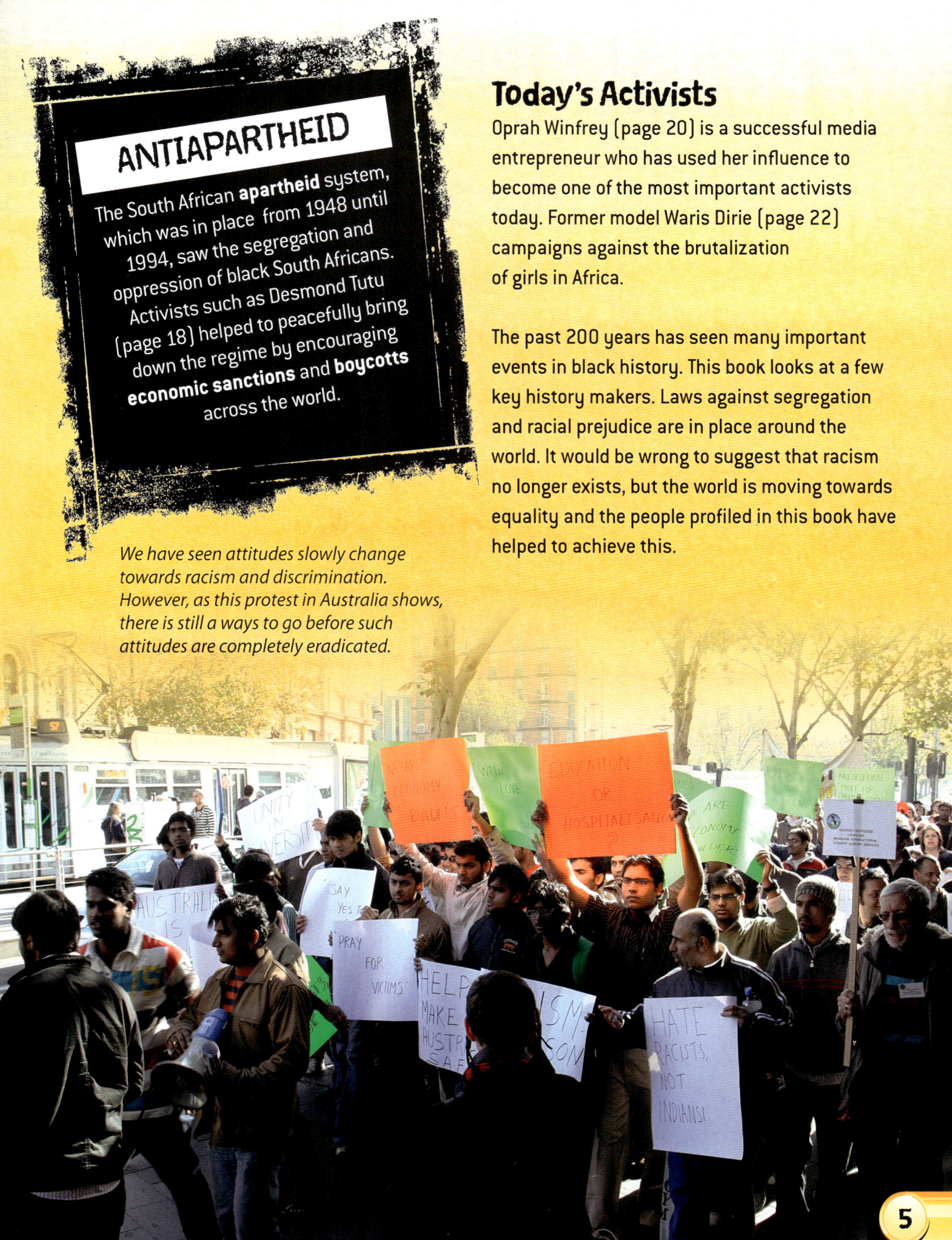

ANTIAPARTHEID

The South African **apartheid** system, which was in place from 1948 until 1994, saw the segregation and oppression of black South Africans. Activists such as Desmond Tutu (page 18) helped to peacefully bring down the regime by encouraging **economic sanctions** and **boycotts** across the world.

We have seen attitudes slowly change towards racism and discrimination. However, as this protest in Australia shows, there is still a ways to go before such attitudes are completely eradicated.

Today's Activists

Oprah Winfrey (page 20) is a successful media entrepreneur who has used her influence to become one of the most important activists today. Former model Waris Dirie (page 22) campaigns against the brutalization of girls in Africa.

The past 200 years has seen many important events in black history. This book looks at a few key history makers. Laws against segregation and racial prejudice are in place around the world. It would be wrong to suggest that racism no longer exists, but the world is moving towards equality and the people profiled in this book have helped to achieve this.

Sojourner Truth
Feminist and Abolitionist

Born into Slavery
Sojourner Truth was born Isabella Baumfree. She lived her young life as a slave on a farm in New York state. Her slave owners treated her badly until, in 1827, she fled with her youngest child and escaped to freedom in New York City.

God's Mission
At the age of 46, Isabella changed her name to Sojourner Truth. She believed that God had given her a mission in life, and set out on a journey to spread the truth about women's rights and the abolition of slavery.

A Tireless Campaign
In 1851, while addressing a women's rights convention in Ohio, Truth delivered a famous speech outlining inequalities women faced. Over the next two decades, she spoke before hundreds of audiences. She helped to recruit black soldiers for the Union Army during the Civil War. Truth campaigned tirelessly against segregation until the age of 75.

> " I cannot read a book, but I have as much muscle as any man and can do as much work as any man. I have plowed and reaped and husked and mowed. Can any man do more than that? "
>
> *Sojourner Truth*

Name: Isabella Baumfree (changed her name at the age of 46)

Born: 1797, Swartkill, New York

Died: November 26, 1883

Honors and awards: First black woman to be honored with a statue in Washington, D.C. (2009).

Interesting fact: Truth was 6 feet (1.8 m) tall and strong, so as a slave she was given jobs normally done by men.

During the Civil War, Truth used the money raised by her lectures to buy food and clothing for black soldiers.

Harriet Tubman
Underground Railroad Conductor

Name: Araminta Ross (changed her name after marriage)

Born: 1820, Maryland

Died: March 10, 1913

Honors and awards: Buried with military honors at Fort Hill Cemetery, Auburn, NY.

Interesting fact: Tubman was often called Moses, after the biblical hero who led Israelite slaves to freedom.

Troubled Beginnings
Harriet Tubman was born into slavery. She was regularly beaten by her slave masters and at the age of 12 she was hit with a metal weight. This caused blackouts and headaches for the rest of her life.

Underground Railroad
In 1849, Tubman escaped to freedom in Philadelphia and joined the Underground Railroad. This group helped slaves escape from the Southern states, where slavery was practiced. The "railroad" was a route that slaves traveled at night with the help of "conductors" who guided them from one safe-house to another. Tubman helped hundreds of slaves flee to the North this way.

Civil War
When the Civil War began in 1861, Tubman worked for the Union Army. She was the first woman to lead an armed raid. In 1863, she freed more than 700 slaves at a battle at the Combahee River in South Carolina. Tubman continued to campaign for the freedom of African Americans until her death in 1913.

During the Civil War, Tubman worked for the Union Army as a cook, a nurse, and a spy!

> "I freed a thousand slaves. I could have freed a thousand more if only they knew they were slaves."
>
> *Harriet Tubman*

Mary Seacole
The War Nurse

Name: Mary Jane Grant (changed her last name after marriage)

Born: 1805, Kingston, Jamaica

Died: May 14, 1881

Honors and awards: A statue will be built in her honor outside St. Thomas's hospital in London.

Interesting fact: Seacole treated members of the British royal family.

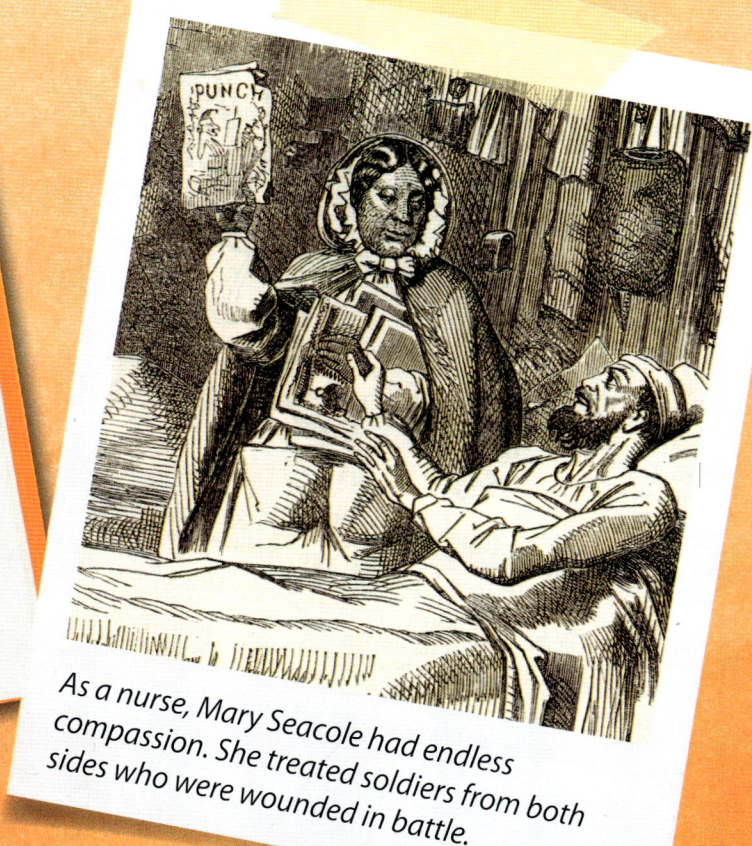

As a nurse, Mary Seacole had endless compassion. She treated soldiers from both sides who were wounded in battle.

Healing Hands

When Mary Seacole was born in 1805, Jamaica was a British **colony**. Her father was a white Scottish soldier in the Army and her mother was a mixed-race, or Creole, healer who treated British soldiers with her herbal medicine. As a girl, Seacole practiced bandaging her dolls. By the age of 12 she was helping her mother treat injured soldiers.

Nursing the Sick

In 1850, there was an outbreak of **cholera** in Jamaica. Although she was not a trained nurse, Seacole cared for many cholera victims, giving them her homemade herbal remedies. Then, in 1851, she traveled to Panama in Central America. In the mosquito-ridden jungle, Seacole bravely rolled up her sleeves and got to work, caring for victims of cholera and **yellow fever**.

The Crimean War

In 1854, the Crimean War broke out in Russia. Seacole asked the British Government to fund her trip to the Crimea to help nurse the wounded, but they refused. Seacole suspected the refusal was on the grounds of her race, so she funded her own trip. In 1855, she set sail for the Crimea.

This portrait of Mary Seacole was painted around 1869. It now hangs in the National Portrait Gallery in London.

In the Crimea, Seacole set up a store with a little hospital above it. The store sold home-cooked food and upstairs she cleaned wounds and applied bandages. On the battlefields, she treated the injured with no concern for the danger around her, often treating soldiers while under gunfire.

Returning Home

When she returned to England, Seacole was in ill health and very poor, so the British press ran a campaign to raise money for her. Today Seacole is still remembered as one of the world's most famous nurses.

MAKING HISTORY

Before the Crimean War, Britain had no trained nurses and nursing was not seen as a worthy job. Mary Seacole changed the way that people thought about nursing forever. In 1860, Britain's first school for nursing was set up at St. Thomas's Hospital in London.

Frederick Douglass
Inspirational Speaker

A Haunting Beginning
Douglass spent his early years with his grandmother, working as a slave. From a young age he witnessed the ill-treatment of slaves by their masters. At the age of 7, Douglass was separated from his grandmother and sent to live with his slave master.

Learning to Read
When Douglass was about 12 years old, his slave mistress taught him to read, even though teaching slaves to read was illegal. He began to read newspapers and books and soon his thoughts on human rights took shape. He started to understand how words could bring about positive change and so began to teach slaves on the plantation to read.

A Great Speaker
Douglass escaped slavery at the age of 20 by impersonating a sailor. He changed his name and began to campaign for the abolition of slavery. Despite being a nervous young man, at the age of 23 Douglass gave an eloquent speech about the life of a slave in front of hundreds of abolitionists. He continued to speak out against slavery and for women's rights until his death in 1895.

Name: Frederick Augustus Washington Bailey (changed his name after escaping slavery)

Born: 1818, Maryland, USA

Died: February 20, 1895

Honors and awards: Appointed Minister of Haiti (1889).

Interesting fact: In his autobiography Douglass states that his father was a white plantation master.

During the Civil War, Douglass became a consultant to President Abraham Lincoln.

Marcus Garvey
Back-to-Africa Movement

In 1919, Garvey set up an ocean liner company to transport black people from America to Africa.

Name: Marcus Mosiah Garvey Jr.

Born: August 17, 1887, Jamaica

Died: June 10, 1940

Honors and awards: National Hero of Jamaica (1964).

Interesting fact: Garvey's beliefs influenced the **Rastafari movement** and he is often mentioned in **reggae** music.

Early Life
Marcus Garvey was born in Jamaica, the youngest of 11 children. As he grew up, he became very aware of the racial discrimination in Jamaican society. This sparked Garvey's lifelong interest in politics and social issues.

Leaving Jamaica
In 1910, Garvey left Jamaica to work on his uncle's banana plantation in Costa Rica. He saw how his fellow black people were being treated and resolved to change things. In the early twentieth century, African Americans experienced poverty and prejudice. Garvey founded the Universal Negro Improvement Association (UNIA) to empower them. He argued that black people should unite and move back to Africa to form a powerful nation.

A Radical Speaker
Garvey had a **radical** approach to campaigning. His **inflammatory** speeches could cause crowd hysteria as he urged African Americans to return to Africa. This was called the Back-to-Africa movement. Though he led a determined campaign throughout his life, Garvey never actually set foot in Africa himself.

Rosa Parks
Mother of the Civil Rights Movement

Rosa Parks grew up on her grandparents' farm in Alabama. African Americans in the area were terrorized by a group of white **supremacists** called the **Ku Klux Klan**, who burned down homes and murdered innocent people.

Family life was hard for Parks, but she left the farm in 1924 when she enrolled at a private girls' school in Montgomery. There she began to train as a teacher. However, she was unable to graduate because she had to return home to look after her grandmother, who had become unwell.

Name: Rosa Louise McCauley (changed her name after marriage)

Born: February 4, 1913, Tuskegee, Alabama

Died: October 24, 2005

Honors and awards: Congressional Gold Medal (1999).

Interesting fact: When Parks was young, she spent only five months of the year at school. The rest of the year she worked in the cotton fields.

Rosa Parks continued to campaign for racial equality until her death in 2005 at the age of 92.

The NAACP

Rosa married a civil rights worker called Raymond Parks in 1932. Together they joined the National Association for the Advancement of Colored People (NAACP), fighting for black people's right to vote. After the Civil War ended in 1865, the Southern states had promised to grant black people rights, including the right to vote. However, racial segregation meant that African Americans were treated as second-class citizens. They did not have the same rights and privileges as white Americans.

> "By the time I was six, I was old enough to realize that we were not actually free... I had a very strong sense of what was fair."
> — Rosa Parks

This photo shows a reenactment of that momentous day in 1955, when Rosa Parks refused to give up her seat on the bus. Her act of protest changed America forever.

Bus Boycott

Both Rosa and Raymond Parks were active members of the NAACP. Rosa's greatest contribution to the civil rights movement happened on December 1, 1955. At that time, the Montgomery bus company segregated black and white riders with separate seating areas, but black people were often required to stand. On that day, the bus driver asked Parks to stand to allow a white passenger to sit down. When Parks refused she was arrested and jailed.

Law Changes

On December 5, 1955, with the help of a young civil rights activist named Martin Luther King Jr. (page 16), the black people of Montgomery, Alabama, decided to stand up for their rights. They began a boycott of the bus system which lasted 381 days, until the Supreme Court ruled that Montgomery's segregated buses were unconstitutional. This was a big victory for the civil rights movement.

Malcolm X
Black Nationalist

Name: Malcolm Little (changed his last name to X in 1952)

Born: May 19, 1925, Omaha, Nebraska

Died: February 21, 1965

Honors and awards: His life has been portrayed in print and on stage and screen, including *The Autobiography of Malcolm X* by Alex Hayley and Spike Lee's 1992 film *Malcolm X*.

Interesting fact: Malcolm was always very disciplined. After his troubled early days, he never smoked or drank alcohol.

After his assassination in 1965, Malcolm X became a cult figure, particularly among young African Americans.

Early Memories

One of Malcolm X's earliest memories was watching his family home burn down. The Ku Klux Klan terrorized his family for their activism in the local black community. When his father was killed in 1931, it was rumored that the Klan were to blame. With his father no longer around, the young Malcolm fell in with the wrong crowd and ended up involved with gamblers and thieves. In 1946, he was sentenced to prison for 10 years.

Moving On

In prison, Malcolm X discovered the Nation of Islam. This Muslim group believed in the superiority of black people over white people. Upon his release, Malcolm X began to give fiery speeches and became the group's leader in 1952. He was critical of white America and preached black **supremacy**, believing that part of the United States should become a separate nation for black people. He said that if necessary African Americans should use violence against white people to regain their position in society.

> "The common goal of 22 million Afro-Americans is respect as human beings, the God-given right to be a human being. Our common goal is to obtain the human rights that America has been denying us."
>
> Malcolm X, August 25, 1964

A Change of Heart

In 1964, Malcolm X's beliefs changed and he left the Nation of Islam. He now believed that all races should live together peacefully. He traveled through the Middle East and Africa, preaching peace. However, many of his old followers disagreed with his new ideas and, in February 1965, he was **assassinated** while attending a rally in New York.

Malcolm X urged his followers to defend themselves "by any means necessary." Here, he is addressing a crowd at a black Muslim rally in New York City, 1963.

MAKING HISTORY

Malcolm X raised **black consciousness** among African Americans, which encouraged them to reconnect with their African heritage and to take control of their lives. Malcolm X became a pop culture icon when rap and hip-hop artists began to use his image on album covers and music videos.

15

Martin Luther King Jr.
Civil Rights Hero

A Good Start
Martin Luther King Jr. was born in 1929 and grew up in relative wealth compared to many African Americans. He wanted to be a minister as he thought it was a strong position from which to fight racism. He became the pastor of a church in Montgomery, Alabama. It was here that he showed the first signs of being a great inspirational public speaker.

Southern States
Before the 1950s, segregation was in force in the Southern states. Black people attended different schools, were segregated on buses and attended different restaurants and cinemas. The civil rights movement began in 1951 to fight this inequality and Martin Luther King Jr. became one of its most influential leaders.

Bus Boycott
In 1955, King became President of the Montgomery Improvement Association (MIA). The organization supported Rosa Parks when she was arrested for refusing to give up her seat to a white passenger. The MIA led the Montgomery Bus Boycott, which forced a change in the law and made it illegal to segregate black and white passengers.

Name: Martin Luther King Jr.

Born: January 15, 1929, Atlanta, Georgia

Died: April 4, 1968

Honors and awards: 1964 Nobel Peace Prize.

Interesting fact: He deeply admired Gandhi, the Indian leader who used nonviolent protest to fight against British rule.

Martin Luther King Jr. encouraged nonviolent protest, through boycotts, demonstrations, and freedom marches.

Assassination

King's views on nonviolent protest were not popular with everyone. Many African Americans thought more extreme action was needed. Meanwhile, white supremacists firebombed his house. The day after a passionate demonstration in support of a strike in Memphis, Tennessee, he was shot and killed while standing on a hotel balcony. His body now lies in the Martin Luther King Jr. Center for Nonviolent Social Change.

MAKING HISTORY

Martin Luther King Jr. played an important role in ending segregation in the United States. Every year, on the third Monday in January, Martin Luther King day is celebrated as a national holiday.

In August 1963, Martin Luther King gave his "I Have a Dream" speech in Washington, D.C., to a crowd of 200,000 people.

Archbishop Desmond Tutu
Antiapartheid Activist

A Tolerant Family

Desmond Tutu was born in Klerksdorp, South Africa. His father was a teacher and his mother a domestic worker. He was raised in a tolerant, peace-loving home. At the age of 12, Tutu's family moved to Johannesburg. At school, he wanted to be a doctor but his family could not afford it, so instead he trained as a teacher.

Full name: Desmond Mpilo Tutu

Born: October 7, 1931, Klerksolorp, South Africa

Honors and awards: First black Archbishop of Cape Town (1984). Nobel Peace Prize (1984). Presidential Medal of Freedom (2009).

Interesting fact: In 1975, Desmond Tutu was appointed Dean of St. Mary's Cathedral in Johannesburg, South Africa. He was the first black person to hold the position.

> " Never will white people hear what we are trying to say? Please, all we are asking you to do is to recognize that we are humans, too. "
>
> *Desmond Tutu*

Desmond Tutu put forward the idea of South Africa as the "Rainbow Nation" in which all races would live in peace.

Religion

Tutu decided he did not want to teach and in 1958 he left the profession to study theology. He was ordained as an Anglican minister in 1961. He became the Archbishop of Cape Town in 1986.

18

Antiapartheid

In 1978, Tutu became the general secretary of the South African Council of Churches. In this role he was a leading spokesman for the rights of black South Africans. The apartheid regime, introduced in 1948, meant that black and white South Africans were required to live separately. Black people were not allowed to vote or travel and interracial marriage was illegal.

In the 1980s, Tutu spoke out against apartheid, bringing the world's attention to the suffering of black South Africans. He encouraged nonviolent action to stop the regime and an economic boycott of South Africa. Soon, so many countries of the world were using boycotts to put economic pressure on the South African government that it ended apartheid.

Voice of Peace

Tutu used his position to speak out against apartheid. Today he is a powerful voice for peace and justice all over the world.

Throughout the 1980s Desmond Tutu traveled around the world, speaking out against apartheid.

MAKING HISTORY

Tutu was highly influential in bringing down the apartheid system. He encouraged economic boycotts from countries all over the world. The boycotts forced the South African government to make changes to its laws.

Oprah Winfrey
Modern Campaigner

Oprah Winfrey was an intelligent child who, even at the young age of three, loved to be on stage and sing in church. However, Winfrey suffered sexual abuse in the family home and at the age of 13 she ran away. She became pregnant at 14 but her son died in infancy.

Name: Oprah Gail Winfrey

Born: January 29, 1954, Kosciusko, Mississippi

Honors and awards: Since 2004 she has been a fixture on *Time* magazine's "100 Most Influential People in the World" list.

Interesting fact: Winfrey's appearance in the film *The Color Purple* (1985), earned her an Oscar nomination.

One of America's most-loved TV celebrities, Winfrey's commitment to the education and empowerment of women and children is tireless and ongoing.

Career Takes Off

Winfrey's broadcasting career began at age 17, when she was employed by a Nashville radio station to read the news. She studied communications in college, and pursued a career in television. She worked in local television in various cities in the United States. In 1985, *The Oprah Winfrey Show* began. A year later it was the number one television show in America.

Oprah's Angel Network

Since the early 1990s, Winfrey has campaigned in favor of a database of convicted child abusers. In 1998, she set up Oprah's Angel Network to encourage TV viewers to use their lives to help others. The network raised $80 million and has funded good causes all over the world.

Leadership for Girls

Winfrey established her Leadership Academy Foundation during a visit to South Africa in 2002. In 2007, she opened a state-of-the-art school that fosters high standards of achievement for girls from impoverished backgrounds. She has also pledged funds to South African orphanages and rural schools, with 50,000 children receiving food, clothing, books, and toys. Winfrey was the first African American woman to become a billionaire. She is now using her fame and wealth to support and help people all over the world.

Winfrey talks to students at the Oprah Winfrey Leadership Academy for Girls in Gauteng, South Africa in 2009.

> "It doesn't matter who you are or where you come from. The ability to triumph begins with you. Always."
>
> Oprah Winfrey

MAKING HISTORY

The 1993 the National Child Protection Act, or "Oprah Bill" was passed. It established a database of convicted child abusers which is now available to law enforcement agencies across America. Her charitable projects and grants continue to support women, children, and families across the world.

Other Activists

Jesse Jackson (1941–)
Born in South Carolina, Jackson won a scholarship to the University of Illinois where he hoped to escape the discrimination of the South. He became a leader in the civil rights movement, encouraging protests and boycotts. Jackson traveled the US promising a "rainbow coalition" of black and white leaders.

Booker T. Washington (1856–1915)
Booker Taliaferro Washington was born a slave in Virginia. He believed that education was the key to economic freedom and social equality, and so he campaigned tirelessly to reform and improve education for African Americans. In 1881, he became the first leader of the Tuskeegee Institute in Alabama, a teacher's college for African Americans.

She had no equipment and was forced to use crates as desks, and crush berries to make ink for writing. To help raise funds, Bethune and the pupils baked pies to sell. The school grew with the help of investors and today it is known as the Bethune-Cookman University. It now has more than 3,600 students.

Wangari Maathai (1940–2011)
Known as the "tree woman," Wangari Maathai was raised in a Kenyan village. In 1976, she founded the Green Belt Movement. This required women from the villages to plant trees to protect the Kenyan landscape. Her actions had a positive effect on the environment and on the local women, who saw that positive action could change things. In 2002, Maathai was elected to Kenya's parliament and has worked with the United Nations on environmental issues and improving education.

Waris Dirie (1965–)
As a teenager, Somali model, actress, writer, and activist Waris Dirie fled from Somalia to London to avoid an arranged marriage. She worked at McDonald's before starting a modelling career. In 1997, she began to campaign for an end to female genital cutting and was appointed United Nations Special Ambassador for the cause. In 2009, she cofounded the Foundation for Women's Dignity and Rights and raises money for schools and clinics in her native Somalia.

Mary Bethune (1875–1955)
Born to former slaves in South Carolina, Mary Bethune became one of the great educators in U.S. history. At a time when there was little or no education for black people, she single-handedly set up a school in Daytona Beach, Florida, to teach African American girls.

Timeline

1850s–1860s The Underground Railroad system helps free thousands of slaves

1854 The Crimean War begins

1860 St. Thomas's hospital in London sets up Britain's first nursing school

1861–1865 The Civil War

1865 Slavery is officially abolished in the U.S.

1925 Malcolm X is born

1929 Martin Luther King Jr. is born

1948 The system of apartheid begins in South Africa

1951 Start of the civil rights movement in U.S.

1955 Rosa Parks refuses to give up her bus seat

1955–1956 The Montgomery Bus Boycott

1962 Nelson Mandela is imprisoned

1963 Martin Luther King Jr.'s "I Have a Dream" speech, Washington D.C.

1965 The assassination of Malcolm X

1968 The assassination of Martin Luther King Jr.

1990 Nelson Mandela is released from prison.

1994 Apartheid ends. Democratic elections are held for all South African people

2008 Barack Obama is voted the first African American President of the United States

Legacy

The legacies of the activists in this book live on, not only in their achievements but also through the work of their families and followers:

Malcolm X Memorial Foundation: www.malcolmxfoundation.org/MXMF/Welcome.html
Founded in 1971 to commemorate his life and work.

Mary Seacole Statue: http://www.maryseacoleappeal.org.uk/
The memorial appeal hopes to build a statue outside St. Thomas's Hospital in London to recognize all the work Seacole did in her lifetime.

Tutu Foundation UK: http://www.tutufoundationuk.org/
This foundation continues Tutu's work by increasing tolerance and understanding in society and creating links between different cultures.

Glossary

abolitionist (a-buh-LIH-shun-ist) An activist who wants to get rid of slavery.

apartheid (uh-PAR-tyd) A government policy that enforced the separation of black and white people.

assassinated (uh-SA-suh-nayt-ed) Murdered.

black consciousness (BLAK KON-shus-ness) A movement seeking to unite black people and take pride in the black race.

boycott (BOY-kot) To refuse to deal with a country or organization as a form of protest.

cholera (KAH-lur-uh) A disease caused by drinking dirty water.

colony (KAH-luh-nee) A country under the rule of another country.

economic sanction (eh-kuh-NAH-mik SANK-shun) When a country puts trade and financial restrictions on another country.

inflammatory (in-FLAM-uh-tor-ee) Intended to create anrgy or violent feelings.

Ku Klux Klan (KOO KLUX KLAN) A secret society of white southerners, who terrorize and suppress black people.

oppression (uh-PREH-shun) Exerting a form of power over another group.

petition (puh-TIH-shun) A written document, signed by a lot of people, to try to demand action from a government or other authority.

plantation (plan-TAY-shun) A large estate or farm where crops are grown.

radical (RA-dih-kul) A person with extreme views.

Rastafari movement (ros-tuh-FAR-ee MOOV-ment) A form of religion that originated in Jamaica and regards Haile Selassie (or "Ras Tafari"), the former emperor of Ethiopia, as God.

reggae (REH-gay) A style of music, originating in Jamaica.

segregation (seh-grih-GAY-shun) To separate or set apart.

supremacy (soo-PREM-uh-see) Having the highest power or authority.

supremacist (soo-PREM-uh-sist) A person who believes in the supreme power of a particular group.

yellow fever (YEH-low FEE-ver) A deadly virus, passed on by mosquitoes.

Index

A
Africa 11, 15
African American 7, 11, 14, 15, 16, 17, 21, 22
apartheid 5, 18, 19, 23

B
Back-to-Africa Movement 11
Bethune, Mary 22

C
civil rights 4, 12, 13, 16, 23
Civil War 4, 6, 7, 10, 23
Crimean War 8, 23

D
Dirie, Waris 5, 22
Douglass, Frederick 4, 10

E
environmental issues 4, 5, 22

G
Garvey, Marcus 11

J
Jackson, Jesse 22
Jamaica 8, 11

K
King, Martin Luther 4, 13, 16–17, 23
Ku Klux Klan 12, 14

M
Maathai, Wangari 5, 22
Montgomery Improvement Association 16

N
National Association for the Advancement of Colored People 12, 13
Nation of Islam 15

O
Oprah's Angel Network 18
"Oprah Bill" 21

P
Panama 8
Parks, Rosa 12–13, 16, 23

R
racism 4, 5

S
Seacole, Mary 8–9
segregation 4, 5, 6, 16
slave 4, 7, 22
slavery 4, 6, 7, 10, 23
St. Thomas's hospital 8, 9, 23

T
Truth, Sojourner 4, 6
Tubman, Harriet 4, 7
Tutu, Desmond 5, 18–19

U
Underground Railroad 4, 7, 23
United Kingdom 8, 9
United States of America 4, 6, 10, 12, 13, 14, 16, 20, 21, 22, 23

W
Washington, Booker T. 22
Winfrey, Oprah 5, 20–21
women's rights 6, 22

X
X, Malcolm 4, 14–15, 23

24